This Little Tiger book belongs to:

_____

_____

_____

For Joey and Kitty ~ A W

LITTLE TIGER
An imprint of Little Tiger Press Limited
1 Coda Studios, 189 Munster Road, London SW6 6AW
Imported into the EEA by Penguin Random House Ireland,
Morrison Chambers, 32 Nassau Street, Dublin D02 YH68
www.littletiger.co.uk

First published in Great Britain 2008
This edition published 2016

A CIP catalogue record for this book is available from the British Library

Printed in China • LTP/1400/5171/0523

10 9 8 7 6 5 4

One Magical Christmas

Alice Wood

LITTLE TIGER
LONDON

It was Christmas Eve in the workshop and
Father Christmas was loading up the sleigh.
    Teddy was worried. "Do you think we'll like
our new home?" he asked.
    "Of course we will!" said Dolly. "It will be wonderful!"

At last the sleigh was full and they were on their way!

Dolly and Teddy peered over the edge
as they flew up, up into the night sky.
The snow was sparkling on the ground below,
and the stars shone brightly above them.

As they soared towards the first house, Teddy's scarf
caught in the wind and whipped away into the night.

"Oh no!" he gasped.

As soon as they had landed, he leaped down and raced after it.

"Come back, Teddy! Come back!" cried Dolly. "Father Christmas will be leaving again soon!"

But Teddy didn't stop.
He chased, jumped and
reached out his paws until
at last he caught the scarf.

"Quick, Teddy!" said Dolly,
and they hurried back
towards the sleigh.

But the sleigh had left without them.

"Father Christmas! Stop! Come back!"
they cried.

But Father Christmas didn't hear them.
It was too late. They were all alone in
the strange, dark woods.

"Oh no!" sobbed Teddy.
"We'll never find our
new home now. What
are we going to do?"
    Dolly gave him a cuddle.

"We'll have to catch up
with Father Christmas,"
she said, bravely.
Teddy sniffed.
"Come on, we can
do it," said Dolly.
"We'll help each other."

So they set off across
the snow together.

It was hard work.
They were only small,
and everything around
them was so big.

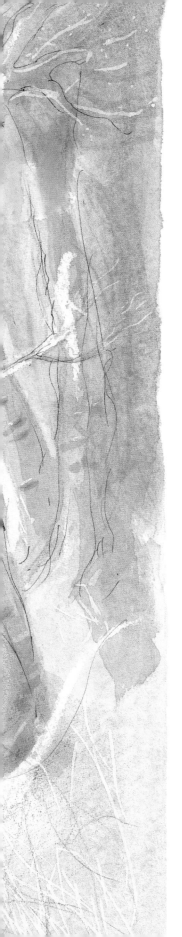

As they walked along, something
tickled Teddy's nose.

"Oh, Dolly!" he giggled. "It's snowing!"

Fluffy snowflakes tumbled down
towards their smiling faces. Dolly tried
to catch them on her tongue.

Teddy built a Snowbear.

"Come on," Dolly said after a while,
"we need to keep going."

It was getting very late. The snow fell thicker. The sky grew darker. The wind blew harder.

Dolly and Teddy struggled along in the deep snow.

Suddenly, they heard a noise.
  "What was that?" whispered Teddy,
holding onto Dolly tightly.
  They looked up and saw a
dark shape in the tall trees . . .

Whooo!

Whooo!

WHOOO!

"Run!" cried Dolly. And they ran
    like the wind.
        Suddenly, Teddy tripped at the top
        of a hill and, with a slip and a slide and
        a bump, he tumbled all the way down.
        "Oh, Teddy!" Dolly cried. "Are you all right?"
        "I think so," he said, sitting up, his eyes
opening wide. "Look, Dolly!"
        There, flickering through the trees,
was a warm, glowing light.
            "Is it the sleigh?" Teddy asked.
            "No," said Dolly. "I think
            it's a house." So they set
            off to find it.

The house looked so warm and inviting.
There was a big Christmas tree with
fairy lights all over it.

"Oooh!" gasped Teddy. "It looks cosy
in there!"

"Let's go in," said Dolly. "I'm sure
Father Christmas will find us here."

Dolly and Teddy crept into the quiet
house, down the long hallway to the
room with the twinkling Christmas tree.

Under the tree they found two little
beds, so they snuggled down to rest.

"Will we *ever* find our new home?"
asked Teddy.

"Of course we will!" said Dolly, and
they soon fell sound asleep.

Snow settled quietly over the sleeping
houses, and children everywhere dreamed
of the magical toys that Father Christmas
would bring.

In the middle of the night, Father Christmas arrived at the house on the edge of the woods, with the twinkling Christmas tree and the two little stockings. Nobody saw him, and nobody heard him.

When he found the two little toys asleep in their beds, he could not believe his eyes. "Well, how did you two get here?" he wondered. He scratched his head. "Well, well, well. You've found your new home all on your own! It must be **Christmas magic**."

On Christmas morning, two little children raced down the stairs to see what Father Christmas had brought them. Under the tree they found just what they had wished for. There was a cuddly teddy in a soft, green scarf and a smiling dolly in a beautiful, blue dress!

Dolly and Teddy looked at each other and smiled. They had found their new home all on their own. And it really was wonderful!